All the Light We Cannot See: A Novel by Anthony Doerr – Reviewed

By
J.T. Salrich

CONTENTS

About The Author

Anthony Doerr, an American writer of fiction, has recently catapulted into the public eye, with this book a 2014 Pulitzer Prize Winner.

Doerr has won many awards for his work and short stories, as well as writing a regular column on science books for the Boston Globe and a contributor to the online magazine, 'The Morning News.'

Born and raised In Cleveland, Ohio, after completing college, he went on to major in History at Bowden College, In Brunswick Maine. He later received an MFA from Bowling Green State University for his services to Literature. Today he lives in Boise, Idaho with his wife and two sons.

Doerr's first published book was a collection of short stories called *Shell Collector* (2002), where most of the stories take place in Africa and New Zealand, where he has previously worked and lived. Doerr wrote another book of short stories called *Memory Wall* (2010).

His first novel, *About Grace*, was released in 2004. Doerr then went on to write a memoir; *Four Seasons in Rome: On Twins, Insomnia and the Biggest Funeral in the History of the World* which was published in 2007.

All the Light We Cannot See is Doerr's second novel and was first published in 2014. It received significant critical acclaim and was a finalist for the *National Book Award for Fiction.*

The book was an also a *New York Times* bestseller and was named by the newspaper as one of the most notable books of 2014.

Themes

The light You Cannot See

You don't have to look far for the key themes in this story (The clue is in the title) There are many things which literally cannot be seen in this book.

Let's take a look. Marie a main character has lost her sight and relies on the guiding light that is her father, to explore the world.

Werner, another main character is metaphorically blinded by his naivety and chooses not to see what is right in front him. His sister Jutta, one of his most trusted allies in life tries to warn him of the rumors she has heard of the "Devil Germans." She knows what the world thinks of Germany, she hears it on the wireless at night, on the foreign broadcast news shows, which she shouldn't be listening to.

"The light at the end of the tunnel" can be hard to see, especially when the characters of this book have so much destruction and death all around them.

Communication

The radio is the key symbol of the theme communication. The radio connects people all around the world and transports messages, of war, whether it be the brainwashing of German youth or delivering of co-ordinates to the French resistance. It was a powerful tool used in the war. A time before mobiles and internet.

Where messages get transmitted into the atmosphere and can be picked up by anyone who is listening.

Radio broadcasting was a propaganda tool for Hitler and the Third Reich. Control the airways, control the minds of the people, is the key phrase!

Radios during the war were banned for fear of an uprising. We see how this idea is explored in the book when gun positions in Saint Marlo are broadcast in code to the French Resistance.

World War II and its victories were partly won with the advancement and design of the wireless and the radio transmitter. Germany being the leaders in this technology. We see this as Werner spends all his nights in the laboratory of Dr. Hauptmann, designing a triangulating transmitter, which can locate the position of enemy antennas.

We see the radio being used as a means of escapism too for our young characters. Werner masters the mechanics of the radio from aged eight and uses his skills as a way of escaping a life in the mines.

At the children's home they listen to stories and songs at night, which drifts the miles away from the imminent presence of war and their normal daily life at the orphanage.

The broadcasts made by Marie's grandfather make a huge impression on Werner. He loses himself completely when he hears the French professor's voice.

Twenty Thousand Leagues under the Sea

Marie is captivated by the book "Twenty Thousand Leagues under the Sea" and retreats into its story, when the world gets too tough to handle, for a girl of her age. The character of Captain Nemo, who spends most of his adult life living in a submarine he built himself, mirrors, uncle Etienne, who after losing his brother in World War I, has for the past Twenty Four years shut himself away in his house.

Geometry and Shapes

There is an important use of numbers and shapes in this story. Triangles are the main basis for the success of the radio transmitter Werner designs to track down enemy radio broadcasts. We also see lots of references to shapes in nature. The pattern of sea shells and the spirals of pine cones for example.

In fact spirals are a prominent shape we see throughout the book; from brain-damaged Frederick's drawings of spirals to Marie's chosen resistance name "Whelk," another type of sea shell.

Good V Evil

The question "Am I doing good or bad?" is a constant moral dilemma for the characters of this book. Werner believes that by leaving the children's home he is doing some good with his life, but objects to the morally wrong things he witnesses around him at his school.

Marie's father takes on his duty as a good employee by agreeing to transport the "Sea of Flames" stone, but somehow is he is a bad father by putting their life at risk?

Marie helps her uncle get the co-ordinates from the bakers, which he transmits on his radio to resistance fighters. Marie questions if she is actually part of something more sinister, like the killing of people.

Are the American pilot's the good guys or the bad guys when they bomb a whole city known to still house civilians?

Fear

War obviously brings out huge elements of fear in most of our main characters and they all go through their own personal fears.

Marie at first fears the blindness that suddenly engulfs her, the rapidly changing world around her, the loss of her father and the changes she has no control over.

Werner fears wasting his life at the children's home, being put to work in the mines. Von Rumpel fears the cancer that is invading his body.

Uncle Etienne has not left his house for Twenty Four years, as he fears the lack of control that comes with interacting with the world.

All the characters are trying to overcome some sort of fear in this book. It's strange how war can do that to you.

Symbolism

The Sea Of Flames

The One Hundred and Thirty Three caret diamond with its legend of eternal life for whoever possesses it, but with the consequence that it will curse all those around you is a symbol of greed, longevity and consequence.

We see Von Rumpel hunting down the stone with a desire to cure his cancer, never giving up hope that he will find the stone, even when he can barely move due to his sickness.

The Radio

We have already talked about the importance communication as a theme in this book. The radio is the key symbol for this theme.

In a world before television, the radio of World War II had the ability to move people and evoke emotion or change of some kind.

The radio allows people to escape mentally from the atrocities surrounding them. We see Werner, who is a master in electronics and circuits and how his world melts away when he works with the inside of a radio.

Marie and her uncle lose themselves in music and are able to dance their problems away in the candlelight.

Both sides of the war machine use transmissions to better their advantage. The Germans rely heavily on brainwashing and propaganda and the resistance use it as a tool to target their enemies' positions.

There is a big sound scape backdrop for this book, with Marie's sense of sound being heightened and the radio static echo's always in the air.

Without the static there is nothing. The static is a symbol of hope.

Numbers

Numbers play a big role for both our main characters. Marie uses numbers to plot out her journeys, locating items and for counting objects around her. She is forever counting as a guide for time also.

Werner has an aptitude for Math and relies heavily on equations to get his Transmitter working.

Numbers can be seen as the symbol of order and safety. Marie feels safe when she knows the exact route of a journey, even in the house. She counts everything in paces.

Werner is most at ease in solving his Math equations, which allow him to slip away from the harsh realities of the world.

Settings

The main action happens simultaneously between France and Germany between 1934 – 1944, and centers on the events of World War II.

Saint Marlo
A city sat on the edge of the sea, on the north coast of France and home to Uncle Etienne. It is also the town where Werner and Marie briefly cross paths before they carry on with their own life destinies.

Paris
Marie-Laure LeBlanc lived in Paris as a child and returns after the war, with her uncle Etienne. The Museum of Natural History is also in Paris and where Marie's father works as a Master Locksmith.

A mining town In Germany
Zollverein is a four-thousand-acre coal-mining complex outside Essen, Germany and home to the orphanage where Werner and his Sister Jutta lived as children.

Hotel of the Bee's
L'hôtel des Abeilles where Werner Pfennig is stationed in Saint Marlo with Frank Volkheimer.

Number 4 rue Vauborel
A tall house in the town of Saint Marlo and home to Marie's reclusive Uncle Etienne and Madame Manec, Etienne's lifelong house keeper.

Summary

The book has two main protagonists Marie, a young French girl who lives in Paris before the war with her father the main locksmith at the Museum of Natural History and Werner a German orphan boy, who has an aptitude for electronics and is forced into Hitler's army.

Marie loses her sight due to congenital cataracts and is her father's shadow as he tends to his work at the Museum. Her father is a master carpenter and carves her an intricate model of their neighborhood to help her navigate her world.

When Marie is aged Twelve, Paris is invaded by the Nazis and she and her father are forced to flee the city, first to a town where her father hopes to deliver a rare and precious stone called the "Sea of Flames" to a contact of the Museums. Unfortunately the house is burnt out when they arrive and they have to head to the walled city of Saint Marlo, to hide out at her uncle Etienne's home.

Werner lives in a children's home in a mining town in Germany, where he spends most of his day with his sister Jutta. Werner finds a radio one day in a rubbish dump and becomes an instant expert in fixing and building circuits.

His talent is spotted by a German colonel and he gains a place at a boy's academy for Hitler Youth. Whilst there he builds a special transmitter which can triangulate the positions of enemy broadcasts.

Werner gets dragged into the heart of the war machine and is aware of the cost of his intelligence operations, which lead him to search for resistance broadcasts in the walled city of Saint Marlo where he eventually crosses paths with Marie, as they try to escape a city under siege from the American bombers.

Marie never gets to see her father again and after the war goes back to Paris with her Uncle Etienne, to live in the apartment where she spent her childhood.

Werner meets his fate one night when he walks out of an American field hospital into a landmine, which kills him instantly.

Part Zero: 7 August 1944

What Happens

We open the story two months past D-day and half of western France has been liberated, but not the coastal walled city of Saint Marlo, a last German stronghold.

Leaflets pour from the sky, warning the last Inhabitants to leave the city for open country immediately.

In the corner of the city at number 4 rue Vauborel, Marie-Laure Le Blanc, a blind Sixteen year old girl, kneels over an intricate model her father built for her of the city. She is waiting for her great Uncle Etienne to return home. He went out the previous evening as she slept and has not since returned.

The drone of the planes grows closer. The sirens start to sound. She should be heading to the basement for shelter, but she just sits and runs her fingers along the model of the streets she has walked so many times before.

Five streets to the north of number 4 rue Vauborel, In a room in L'hôtel des Abeilles, a young Eighteen year old German private by the name of Werner Pfennig, wakes to the sound of an anti-air corporal telling him to "Get to the cellar." For the past Four weeks the hotel has been turned into a fortress by a detachment of Austrian Anti-Airmen. They install an anti-air gun named "Gun 88" on the fourth floor, which can fire twenty-one-and-a-half-pound shells nine miles away.

On an Island not far from the city, a fortress called National are the home to three hundred and eighty French prisoners of war. They all scan the moonlit sky looking for what they know will soon appear. The bombs.

Marie-Laure clutches a tiny stone in one hand. A dozen American Bombers roar towards her. The floor starts to throb under her knees "Papa?" she whispers in fear. But he is not there. She is all alone.

Analysis

Part Zero is the calm before the storm and sets the scene for the destruction that is about to happen, as the city is due to get bombed by the Americans fighter pilots, any time soon. We meet our main characters who share the same fate, both hiding out in buildings only three streets away from each other.

Study Questions

1. What Important Information have we already learned about our main characters Marie-Laure Le Blanc and Werner Pfennig?
2. How does this opening part help to build tension for the rest of the story?

Important Terms/ Characters

Werner Pfennig: An eighteen year old German private.

Marie-Laure Le Blanc: A sixteen year old blind girl, staying at her Uncle Etienne's home.

Uncle Etienne: Marie's uncle.

Quotations

"American artillery units drop incendiary rounds into the mouths of Mortars"

Part One: 1934

What Happens

We meet Marie-Laure Le Blanc again, but now she is six-years old and lives in an apartment in Paris, with her father who is the principle locksmith at the Museum *National d?istoire Naturelle.* Her mother died in childbirth.

Marie's eyesight is deteriorating and within a month she will be blind, from congenital cataracts. The doctors say it is Incurable.

Marie goes on a children's guided tour of the museum one day where the guide tells the children the story of the "Sea of Flames," a precious, but also cursed stone apparently kept locked away behind thirteen locked doors to apparently protect people from its power. Every owner of the stone has encountered long life, but tragedy and death to the people all around them.

Marie's father starts to school his daughter and carves her a replica of their neighborhood so she can learn to navigate it alone. He takes her to work at the museum every day and quizzes her about the locations, look and feel of artifacts.

They work on her Braille workbook and he carves her puzzle boxes for her birthday, which she solves with ease. On her ninth birthday her father gives her a book in Braille. It is "Around the World in 80 Days" an instant hit with Marie, who blocks out the world around her and loses herself in its words.

We meet Werner Pfennig, he is Seven years old and raised along with his younger sister Jutter aged Four years, at an orphanage in Zollverein: a four-thousand-acre coal-mining complex outside Essen, Germany. He is bright, cheerful and inquisitive despite the economic decay happening all around him.

A year passes and Werner finds a broken radio in the rubbish dump and meticulously pieces it back together, until it works again. At night the children of the home sit and listen intently to music, plays, stories and political broadcasts about the rise of a new stronger Germany.

One day an official from the Labour Ministry comes to the home, to inform them that all children will go to work at the mine when they turn 15. Werner is fearful of the mines. His father died at Pit 9 in the mines. Sometimes he tows Jutta there to show her where their father died.

At night Werner loses himself in his favorite radio program, A French professor who speaks with passion about the things Werner likes the most; Science, Mathematics and History. The professor's message resonates with Werner;

"Open your eyes and see what you can with them before they close forever."

The rumors of the Germans invading is circulating in Paris. But life goes on. Marie and her father go to work at the museum. She can smell the approaching machines, the gasoline on the wind. Marie senses something is changing.

Werner is now enrolled into the "State Youth" as all boys of his age. He thinks of the importance of the world outside Zollverine. He loves to build and fix things and becomes known as the "Radio Repairman." He keeps a map within his head of the inner mechanics of a radio.

It's 1940 in Paris and there have been less visitors to the museum and talk of an invasion. Gas masks are being sold in shops. The museum starts to move artefacts out to country estates of the wealthy. Sand bags appear at the gates.

As the first bombs drop and chaos mounts in the street, Marie and her father flee the city on foot.

We learn that Marie's father has a precious stone in his belongings, potentially the "Sea of Flames." The museum director gives four stones to workers to hide. Three decoys and one real stone. Could it really be the real one-hundred-and-thirty-three-carat diamond he carries?

Werner is asked by a corporal to come fix an American radio. Scared that he has been found out for listening to foreign broadcasts, he fixes the radio in a blink of an eye. Impressed the corporal says he will write him a recommendation letter which he must take to the recruiting office in town for a place at one of Hitler's training academies.

When Werner returns home, he takes the radio, which he has had for six years, cherished, modified, fine-tuned and spent night after night lying with his sister Jutta losing themselves in the broadcasts from the French professor. He takes it into the alleyway and smashes it to pieces. He feels it is to protect his sister Jutta, who shouldn't be listening to foreign radio broadcasts, but she can't forgive him for his betrayal.

Analysis

By going back in time, we learn about the history of the two main characters introduced to us in Part Zero.

Marie's life is about to change drastically more than she could ever imagine and it takes a long adjustment of learning to cope with her new darkness in the light.

We are introduced to the characters' world before the war starts.

Werner we learn has an aptitude for electronics and fixing things. Marie loves to solve her father's puzzles and read her Braille books. Both characters jump into fictional worlds to escape the chaos around them, be it the orchestra felling the room from the radio or the words of the "Around the world in Eighty Days."

The times they are changing for our characters. The War is coming.

Study Questions

1. How do Marie and Werner try to escape the approaching war and hold onto their Innocence?
2. Why does Werner smash the radio?
3. What clues are given that Werner is ready to

escape his life at the children's home?

Important Terms/Characters

Daniel Le Blanc: Marie's father

Jutta: Werner's sister

Sea of Flames: A precious diamond kept locked away at the museum.

Quotations

"Open your eyes, concludes the man, and see what you can with them before they close forever"

Part Two: 8 August 1944

What Happens

The story flits between the two locations where Werner and Marie are trapped or hiding.

We are back on the night of the bombing of Saint Marlo. Right in the mist of the action as each bomb pounds down to earth. The story mostly moves though the destruction of the city second by second.

Doors fly away from their frames, slates fall from rooftops into the streets, dust clouds mount to the sky as the twelve bombers quickly realign for another attack. There is fire everywhere, climbing the walls, spilling into the streets like waves from the sea.

"The Hotel of The Bees," where Werner is stationed in the basement is lifted into the sky in a cloud of flames and rains back down to earth piece by piece.

At number 4 rue Vauborel, Marie is crouched in a ball under her bed, crying for her "Papa." She has the "Sea of Flames" stone in one hand and a carved puzzle box in another, she holds them tight. The house shakes and glass and plaster fall to the floor.

As the thundering sound stops, a brief moment of silence is had before she smells a familiar smell, it is smoke, and there is fire. Marie makes her way down the stairs, counting the paces till her next recognizable landmark. She is barefoot as she cannot locate her shoes. She makes it to the basement where she hides in the dark.

Werner is found in the rubble by the giant Frank Volkheimer. He cannot hear the screams, but the roars coming from the bombers overhead move through him. He watches his friend's frantic lips move. The stairs have been blasted away, it is the only way out. His priorities in order are "locate the others, find the radio, get to the exit!"

Analysis

The purpose of this chapter is solely to drag you into the depths of the main event. The siege of Saint Marlo. The story is in the descriptions of the destruction all around and the desperation of our main characters Marie and Werner as they struggle to cling to life. Their survival instincts kick in. The destruction moves quickly, the sound scape is loud and deafening.

Study Questions

1. How does the pace of the action help to draw you into the event?
2. What language is used to describe the deafening sound of the bombing?
3. Talk about the importance of our characters' sensory awareness and how it helps them into survival mode.

Important Terms/Characters

Frank Volkheimer: Werner's friend from college.

Quotations

"Are we dead?" He shouts into the dark "Are we dead??
"A news-stand floats, burning"

Part Three: June 1940

What happens

It is two days after Marie and her father fleeing Paris. Marie is tired and her feet are raw from walking. They arrive in Evreux, where the museum director has given Daniel an address to take the stone to, with a promise of lodging and food. When they arrive at the address on the paper *9 rue St. Nicolas* it is on fire, the owners long gone, fled to London and people are looting the Chateau for prized contents.

The contingency plan is to make their way to Marie's uncle who they say is 76% crazy, Wracrazed mind from World War I. He has a house in the walled city of Saint Marlo. When they reach the city next to the sea a whole bag of new sensations hits Marie; the smell of Sea, salt, bird poo, seagulls and the waves crashing on the shore.

They are welcomed by Madame Manec, a big character who remembers Marie's father (Just) from when he was a boy. She is the keeper of the house and takes good care of Etienne-since he was a boy.

Werner travels to Essen to sit his entrance exam at the National Institute of Education. The tests last six full days and all the candidates have to wear the identical crisp white uniform and answer over one hundred questions about their race and heritage. Werner guesses most of his answers, as he is an Orphan with no link to his past.

Werner is pulled between his desire to escape the drudgery of a life in the mines and leaving his younger sister Jutta behind. She hasn't spoken to him since he broke the radio. She has heard reports of what people think of Hitler and his army and her brother is going to be one of them. Werner feels part of something for once in his life, despite his sister's disapproval.

We meet Sergeant Major Reinhold Von Rumpel, based in Vienna and an expert on Diamonds. He can polish and facet a stone as well as any other Aryan in Europe. Before becoming a Sargent, he was a gemologist who ran an appraisal business out of a second-story shop. Now he is on a mission to find the lost gem stone that is known as "The Sea of Flames."

Marie is bored of being stuck in her uncle's house, not allowed to go outside out of fear. Etienne reads to her often and they share their dreams and make believe worlds. Etienne hasn't left the house in twenty four years.

Werner has impressed his professor so much he is told he will work in the laboratory after dinner every night including Sundays. Werner feels he is a part of something important for once, something beyond himself. He writes home to his sister often telling stories of his adventure, his view of the world and his admiration for his bunk mate Fredrick.

Etienne takes a curious Marie to the locked room on the Fifth floor and behind a concealed entrance inside is a room with a recording studio. We learn before World War I Marie's grandfather would transmit recordings from this room. The same recordings Werner and Jutta would sit up into the early hours listening to on the refurbished radio back at the children's home.

Marie realizes the basis for her uncle's fear of leaving the house stems from the death of his brother in the war. He can't control the outside world, but in his home, he can rekindle some essence of the past with the recordings they made and be safe away from danger.

A perfumer by the name of Claude Levitte, is an opportunist and makes money where there is a market for something. Every day he fills suitcases with meat and boards a train for Paris, where he sells the lot on the black market for a large sum of money. One morning he spots Marie's father measuring the street and marking numbers into a book. He looks suspicious and Claude sees an opportunity. The Germans will want to reward someone handsomely for informing them of strange behavior?

Marie's father receives a telegram to return to the museum in Paris. He will leave Marie with her uncle for 10 days. Should he bring the stone he thinks? He never makes it to Paris and is arrested by plain clothes police, just outside the city and questioned for hours about his tools, the measurements in his book, what are the keys for? They do not believe his story that he is a locksmith, with keys for the Museum and the tools are for a model he has made for his daughter.

They seem to be accusing him of plotting to destroy the Château de Saint-Malo. He is bundled into a lorry with other prisoners destined for Germany. He feels like the border could be the edge of a cliff. What will Marie do without him?

Analysis

The plot really develops in this part, as we head back to a pre-war time frame. We see how Werner and Marie adjust to their new life, away from the places they feel comfort in. They somehow mature in that short space of time.

Each character is on a personal mission and a period of growth. Marie has to be without her father for ten days, the longest she has ever been without him. Werner has left behind his sister Jutta at the Children Home. Frank Volkheimer has made finding the "Sea of Flames" a personal mission. The future is uncertain and you get a sense the characters are oblivious to the mighty war that approaches, although there is fear all around them.

Important Terms/Characters

Etienne: Marie's uncle

Von Rumpel: A trained Gemologist in Hitler's army, scouring Europe is evaluating the jewels and artefacts of dead or imprisoned Jews.

Madame Manec: The longtime family housekeeper of Etienne.

Study Questions

1. Discuss how the theme of fear is apparent with the characters in our story in this part.
2. Discuss the idea that both Marie and her uncle are

trapped within their own worlds.

Quotations

"Never has he felt such a hunger to belong?

"You would like Frederick I think. He sees what other people don't"

Part Four: 8 August 1944

What Happens

We return back to the scene of the bombing of Saint Marlo, hours after the attack. The city is alive with fire and smoke fills the air like a volcano.

We see Von Rumpel is flanked in a fortress thirty minutes from the city. He scans the burning sky for a tall house, number 4 rue Vauborel. Von Rumple is sick, a black vine, he says, is overtaking his body. Before he departs this world he must find the stone "The Sea of Flames." He makes a plan to wait till the smoke is cleared and take his chance.

Werner and Volkheimer his old school buddy, are still trapped in the basement of the hotel. Volkheimer intermittently switches his field light on and off. The radio he fears is broken. The oxygen seems to have depleted from the hole rapidly.

Volkheimer has hope they can fix the radio, but Werner has given up and wishes Volkheimer shot him with his rifle. Volkheimer shakes some sense into him "Think of your sister."

Marie is still hiding out in the basement of her uncle's house. She does not know if her uncle is dead or alive and she fears leaving the basement, in case the Germans have overrun the city above her.

She eventually musters the courage to leave and takes

with her a two cans of food. A trip wire that has been set up at the front door is tripped. Someone is in the house.

Analysis

All our characters are physically trapped in some way, uncertain if they desire to leave their current location out of fear and lack of hope. Do they really want to risk seeing the damage and destruction that has occurred above them? How easy it could be to just cave in and give up on life, especially if you are dying anyway?

Important Terms/Characters

Frank Volkheimer: A giant Aryan, a rank above Werner.

Study Questions

1. Why do you think Von Rumpel hunts the sea of Flames stone? Do you think he believes in its power of longevity?
2. Which characters show their cowardice in this part?

Part Five: January 1941

What Happens

It has been some weeks since Werner's bunk mate
Fredrick was beaten down by the savage cadets at his
school. Fredrick does not have ill feeling for Werner and
invites him home to Berlin, where he has a view into
Fredrick's middle class life before Schulpforta. His life is
a million miles away from the children's home where he
grew up as a boy.

It has been Twenty days since Marie's father left for Paris
and still no word, no letter and the museum says he never
arrived. Where could he be? Marie slips into a depression
and can barely leave her bed as a realization hits her; she
may never see her Papa again. She is angry with the
world. Angry with her father who would always promise
"I will never leave you!"

Madame Manec, proposes that her friends start a silent
group to protest against the Germans in the city. They set
about doing small actions like changing road signs and
putting dog shit on the brothel step.

Werner and the boys at his school are woken in the early
hours of the morning, where they are enticed into
torturing a prisoner to death by throwing ice cold buckets
of water on him. The prisoner is already dead when his
roommate Fredrick refuses to throw another bucket. After
this event Fredrick is tortured daily by his peers and
teachers. The dead body of the prisoner lay in the

courtyard for weeks. Volkheimer lets slip that the prisoner scene happens every year with all the new cadets.

Werner has been working for months on a transmitter which will help triangulate the position of enemy radio broadcasts. It works perfectly and he feels his loyalty is proven, but somehow he feels guilt every time he puts his uniform on.

His friend Fredrick goes missing one morning and he suspects his fate that the cadets have chased him down and beaten him to death.

After weeks of morning her father's disappearance, Madame Manec deciders to take Marie out of the house against Etienne's advice. They go to the ocean, she has never been before. The sound and smell are magnificent.

She recalls stories her uncle has told her about the moon pulling the sea, bombs on the beach. Her father's model of the city did not take in the surrounding ocean and its vastness. Raindrops of sea water hit her face, a knot she had in her stomach dissolves.

When she returns home, she climbs up the five flights to her uncle's room and gives his pockets full of stones, shells, clams and beach artefacts, things from the outside which he does not usually get to see. She goes out every morning with Madame Manec and counts the steps to the beach. She knows the rout perfectly.

Routine has slowly crept back into Marie's life as she follows Madame Manec on her errands. Her connection to her father now lay in the intricate model he made before he left. She runs her fingers over it now with recognition.

Sergeant Major Von Rumpel has information the "Sea of Flames" stone he took from the Museum in Paris is a fake. This does not deter him, in fact, it spurs him on to find the real stone. He gets information that Dunport a Parisian gem dealer made three casts of the stone.

Madame Manec asks Etienne if he can help her with some secret mission against the Germans, by where he can use his radio up in the attic to transmit codes. He doesn't want any part of it. He is happy doing nothing with his life, which Madam Manec cannot understand.

Hubert Bazin, who was helping Madame Manec carry messages has disappeared. Half the ladies stop coming to the secret meetings at Number 4 rue Vauborel for fear of being arrested.

Life at the college is bleak for Werner. Every week a new instructor is swept up into the war machine, the school has become out of control as the cadet's show no respect for the new elderly teachers. Electricity is intermittent food brought on a raged donkey instead of a car as gasoline is pumped into the war machine, but the news circulates that the Germans are doing good and advancing. Propaganda reports fill the airwaves. "We move with astounding speed. Five thousand Seven hundred Russians killed, Forty-Five Germans lost"

Boys at the school constantly get news that their fathers have been killed in the line of duty. At night, the constant sound of the trains moving to the east can be heard, they never stop.

Werner sees how his new bunk mate wants to impress with serious intensity. The new cadets do exactly as they are told, march in unison, and spurt out phrases in unison. No thought, just duty.

French Police come to Marie's uncle's house, to let them know her father is in Germany and has been charged with theft and conspiracy. Etienne bans Madame Manec from having any more meetings in the house and burns the "Free France Flags".

Harold Bazin gives Marie his key to a secret grotto built into the city ramparts that block out the sea. Inside is a protected natural habitat filled with sea creatures. Werner gets orders to serve in the army after it is said there is a discrepancy in his age. It is quite clear he is not a day over fifteen.

Marie's father has sent letters, which start off upbeat and promising, but the last reads as though they will never meet again. He gives clues to a possible gift for Marie in the house.

Madame Munich gets pneumonia and for two weeks is resting up in bed, she seems to recover, but one morning Marie wakes to find her hardly able to move. Women crowd the house and after a while she is taken away on a horse and cart like a sack of potatoes.

Werner goes to see his friend Fredrick who is alive, but unable to remember anything of his past and now confined to a life where he is spoon fed and has no sense of who or where he is. Werner is ashamed and can hardly look at his friend Fredrick, it would have been better maybe if he was dead?

Analysis

This part of the story sees lots of movement and transformation. The war is advancing and the radio delivers news that Germany are winning ground, but the reality around Werner paints another picture entirely, the order that once was is spiraling out of control.

The mood has changed and a sense of the walls and regime crumbling down is apparent. Everyone is swept up into the war machine, whether they like it or not. Werner is given orders to join the war, even though he is just fifteen. Madam Manec holds secret meetings, where she plots against the Germans. Von Rumpel, undeterred is advancing and getting closer to his prize.

Hope is being lost on a daily basis for our characters and there are moral dilemmas to decide. What part will they play in history?

Study Questions

1. How much has Werner changed do you think since leaving the children's home?
2. Compare how Marie and Etienne are both trapped and how they learn to cope with this or not?
3. What clues do we have that Germans are losing the war?
4. Madam Menac asks Etienne "Don't you want to be

alive before you die?" What is meant by this do you think?

Quotations

"Because someone else is doing something, doesn't mean you have to too"

"Rail cars move to the east, they just keep moving"

"Don't you want to be alive before you die?"

Part Six: 8th August 1944

What Happens

We are back at number 4 rue Vauborel, where someone has entered the house and tripped the wire. Marie is alone, so if it is her uncle, he would have called to her by now.
Marie's thoughts are positive, it could be a neighbor, a fireman. She hears her father's voice in her head "A rescuer would be calling for survivors, ma chérie. You have to move. You have to hide."

She is on the third floor. She has her cane, Etienne's coat, and the two cans from the basement, the knife, and the brick. The wooden model house in her dress pocket. The stone inside that. Water in the tub at the end of the hall.

As Marie silently makes her way to the sixth floor, the intruder starts to climb the stairs, she realizes she has heard the out of time walk of this sergeant before.

She finds the door to the huge wardrobe in her grandfather's room and climbs inside to find the fake door leading to the attic.

"Silently" says the voice of her father. She begs for the stone in the house in her pocket to protect her now more than ever.

A million heart beats beat so loud in her chest, she fears the intruder will hear her.

We go back to the basement where Werner and his comrades are stuck. Walter Bernard is now dead. Werner works away on the radio to try and fix it. He manages to pick up some static and he feels like he is Eight years old again in a room with his sister hearing the static for the first time.

When the field light battery dies, he works from memory, he has fixed a hundred radios.

Von Rumpel works his way up to the 5th floor and into the room where Marie sleeps. He has found what he is looking for, the model of the town where he knows the gem should be, from the letters her father has been sending her.

Analysis

Marie is in danger and all alone, with nobody to protect her, now an intruder has broken into the house. The fear sets in, as she makes for the wardrobe that leads to the attic. This part highlights are characters' sense of survival. They must face their fear or die!

Study Questions

1. Do you believe Von Rumpel will not hurt Marie if she is found?
2. How do Marie and Werner channel their fear to try and escape?

Quotations

"Protect me now, stone, if you are a protector"

Part Seven: August 1942

What Happens

Werner leaves the school and is taken on a train to who knows where. He sees train cars hurtle by him with dead and living people squashed in together. He finally arrives at a village and is given a cold reception "Welcome to War" he thinks.

After Madame Manec death, Etienne goes into a brief morning after which he seems to pull himself together to look after Marie and to honor Madam Manec's legacy by carrying on her secret work, transmitting codes to the resistance fighters.

Marie is enthralled at her uncles new found energy and very eager to be part of the plan. She knows the protocol perfectly. She sets off to collect the numbers from the bakers, baked in a loaf of bread and warns her not to stop at the beach, straight home.

Etienne sets to work making traps in case someone unwanted comes to the home and a false door for the wardrobe in his grandfather's room, which conceals the door to the attic, where Etienne broadcasts the resistance numbers. Sometimes he plays a little snippet of some music at the end of each broadcast.

One night he and Marie dance way their troubles in the loft as the music plays, broadcasting out of the house. As Marie loses herself in the happy moment, he realizes this is why he transmits the codes, for that pure look of freedom she has on her face as they dance. He has left the record on too long. The paranoia sends him into his crazy thoughts and he fears the dark horse of death is to visit them at their home.

Volkheimer explains Partisans are attacking the trains and believed to be using radios. They manage to triangulate a position, the transmission is in Russian and they stake out the house where the partisans are hiding. They are killed and Werner is left to rescue any radio equipment and burn the house down. He feels like all roads lead to this point where he has accomplished something and that there is a point in his work.

Etienne and Marie for months now have been transmitting the numbers. They have a routine. Go to the bakers.

"One ordinary loaf, please."
"And how is your uncle?"
"My uncle is well, thank you."

All winter Marie and her uncle go on in this way and Werner keeps on triangulating positions of Partisans.

Marie and Etienne start to get more notes from the bakery from people wanting to let loved ones know they are ok and such. Etienne adds these to the broadcast which take no longer than six minutes.

Etienne reads Marie's father's letters to her and she ponders over the lines "Today I saw an oak tree disguised as a chestnut tree. I know you will do the right thing. If you ever wish to understand, look inside Etienne's house, inside the house." She has yet to find out what it means.

Saint Marlo has been near enough evacuated except for essential personnel. Etienne says they shall not leave, especially now they are doing some good.

Von Rumple's cancer is advancing he has found three fakes of the "Sea of Flames" stones, he knows he is so close to finding the real stone now.

We learn it has been over three years since Marie's father left the house for Paris and Four years since she has read Braille, but on her Sixteenth birthday Etienne gets "Twenty Thousand Leagues Under The Sea: Part Three"

Analysis

Etienne regains his life once Madam Manec dies. Her words of doing something before you die, ring in his head and he proves to uphold her legacy. The power of love can give us strength, as we see here with Etienne and his love for his niece Marie. His desire to do well is strong, they want to help the resistance and end the war. They have something to live for.

Study Questions

1. How can love for another person drive you to be brave?
2. How does Etienne conquer his fear?
3. How much do you think Marie has forgotten her

father?

Quotations

"Don't you want to be alive before you die?"

"The bony figure of Death rides the streets below, stopping his mount now and then to peer into windows"

Part Eight: 9th August 1944

What Happens

We open to this chapter three days after the initial siege on the city. The shelling has lulled to a distant noise and Marie-Laure is not sure how long she has been cooped up in the attic, hiding from the intruder.

Marie is insanely thirsty and her conscious is being pulled by the voice of her father who says *"You must stay where you, do not move"*

She is desperate to open one of the two cans she found in the basement, but her father's voice enters her conscious *"Don't do it Marie, it's too dangerous."* She wrangles back and forth with the voice of her father, but chooses to go ahead and seek the water from the tin to relieve her thirst anyway. We see how Marie has possibly outgrown her father's guidance and is now in survival mode, alone.

As the shells make a more rhythmic pattern above her, she uses the segments of noise to bang down on the can with a knife and stone. After six bashes she has made a significant opening to drown the cool salty water of the beans that lay within.

We go back to Werner and Volkheimer in the basement of the hotel. They are quickly running out of Oxygen and the battery in the radio is nearly dead. Werner tries his best to find a signal, but fails.

Defeated Volkheimer sits with 2 grenades in his lap and Werner thinks how great it would be if they were to go off and Illuminate the darkness that surrounds them.

Marie hears Von Rumpel go downstairs and ponders whether he has gone for good? Should she leave the attic? She must apply logic like her father, like Professor Pierre Aronnax from "Twenty Thousand Leagues Under The Sea. She makes it to the bathroom and back without getting caught and fills herself up with water. She manages to grab her book too.

Marie decides that she will use her uncle's radio to try and seek help, to seek company in her loneliness. Someone must be listening. She raises the Antenna and counts to One Hundred. No-one has come for her. She locates the microphone and switches on the transmitter. Read to me papa? *"You read to me."* he says. Softly she reads from her book "Twenty Thousand Leagues under the Sea"

Day four of being trapped in the basement, Werner ideally pulls the pin along the coils and to his surprise he hears the crisp whispers of Marie. Is he hallucinating? He hears her speak *"He is here. He is right below me."* He must save her.

Analysis

We start to get the feeling our characters are searching for each other as Marie makes a broadcast on her uncle's transmitter and Werner listens to static waiting to hear something. Success, he hears her and now he just has to find her, before Von Rumpel does.

Study Questions

1. How does the radio represent a companion to Werner and Marie when they are all alone?
2. How much do you think the voice he hears remind him of his sister?

Part Nine: May 1944

What Happens

We move back in time and Werner arrives in the walled city of Saint Marlo, still following his orders to fish out the enemies who transmit codes to resistance fighters.

Von Rumpel receives clues to the whereabouts of the stones. He knows they are in Saint Marlo.

One morning as Marie goes to the bakery to fetch the loaf with the resistance codes inside and Madam Ruelle tells her the times are a changing and "Mermaids are coming," code for the Americans are on their way.

Werner picks up Etienne's transmission and recognizes the voice from the broadcasts, it's the voice from his childhood, from the broadcasts he would listen to when he was Eight years old back at the children's home. He does not wake his sleeping comrades to tell them, he is committing treason, but somehow something inside him dances with joy.

"Open your eyes and see what you can with them before they close forever"

A few days pass before Werner works up the courage to go to the house where he has heard the voice in the night, the house with the large antenna aside the chimney breast. Much to his amazement, he finds a beautiful Auburn haired girl who leaves the house and not a grown man as he had expected.

He follows her trying not to be seen before he realizes she cannot see him, she is blind! He follows her all the way to the bakery "Why are his hands shaking? Why can't he hold his breath?"

Marie-Laure puts the loaf in her knapsack, leaves the bakery, and winds toward the ramparts to Hubert Bazin's grotto, only to bump into Von Rumpel. He speaks in French to her, although she knows he is German. Fear of the loaf of bread she carries in her sack, will be found and she, her uncle and Madam Ruelle will be shot dead.

Marie retreats into the safety of the cave and can here Von Rumple's distinctive shuffle on the other side, he promises to go once he has his answers "Did your father leave you anything" he asks and to Marie's surprise, the anger comes out.

"He left me nothing, just a model of this town and a broken promise." Convinced he leaves.

Etienne expects Marie, but after Thirty Four minutes he panics and for the first time in Twenty Four years he leaves the house, dashing to the bakers. She is not there and then he remembers where he and his friends used to play when they were young. In a secret cavern below the ramparts.

He dashes there to find Marie and vows she must never leave the house again and he will take on the duty of getting the bread with the rolled up pieces of paper.

Werner cannot get the girl out of his head, he pictures her perfectly and feels something he has not felt in a long time stir inside him.

Marie thinks "What is the German after?" It's not the antenna, something else. She racks her brain, then remembers the words from her father's letter

"Look inside Etienne's house, inside the house!" Her fingers run across the model till she finds the model of number four rue Vauborel street where she masters the puzzle box and out drops a pearl shaped stone, the Sea of Flames!

Early one morning Etienne leaves the house and doesn't tell Marie why. He will be back soon he promises. He doesn't come back and Marie is alone.

This chapter ends as the story began with white leaflets being dropped from the sky, warning the inhabitants to leave, it is written in French and is freshly printed.

Analysis

This is the first time in the whole story, where all our characters meet and share the same space of time. We can sense that an end is near as they all close in on each other. Marie is alone at the house and in danger. Von Rumpel is coming to find the stone.

Study Questions

1. How important is the stone to Von Rumpel and Marie? Who needs it more?
2. Do you think the feelings Werner feels are love?
3. Why do you think Volkheimer allows Werner to keep the resistance radio broadcast a secret?

Quotations

"Mermaids are coming?"

Part Ten: 12 August 1944

What Happens

Marie continues to read "Twenty Thousand Leagues under the Sea" entwined with calls for help from the men in her life who were meant to protect her. Werner Listens and tells Volkheimer they must escape to help her. He has known all along that he knew of the resistance radio broadcast.

Von Rumbel is still below in the house and after five days of being trapped in her uncle's attic, no food, no water, she is ready to give up and make meet her destiny she puts "Clare Du lune" on the Grammar Phone and turns up the volume.

She knows Von Rumpel will hear. In her mind, she longs back to the Garden Les Plantes, her Father and the museum. Sitting on the top ladder rung and holding a knife, she awaits her fate.

Back at the Hotel of the Bee's, Volkheimer builds a barrier, to protect him and Werner so he can pull a grenade. It has worked and they are not dead. They climb out and Volkheimer tells Werner with tenderness to go and save the girl, to save Marie.

Von Rumpel is about to climb into the wardrobe when he hears the chimes of the trip wire and someone enter the house-this must be Werner.

Werner heads directly to the top of the house, he knows she will be near the antenna. He reaches the fifth floor landing and is met by Von Rumpel, who confides he knows what he is looking for and where to find it.

Werner has placed his rifle next to Marie's bed and is threatened by Von Rumpel who pulls his own rifle and aims it at Werner, we assume to kill him. Suddenly there is a crash from the room with the large wardrobe and Von Rumpel drops his aim for a second, enough time for Werner to grab Volkheimer rifle and kill him dead as the whole world seems to suck in on its self.

Werner meets the voice of the girl he has been intently listening to for days now. She opens the wardrobe door and is told he can get her out of the city at 12pm when there is a ceasefire. They share water and a tin of Madam Manec's delicious peaches. For a moment life is good. As shells scream over the house, he thinks only that he would like to sit there with her for a thousand years.

Werner shares that he and his sister Jutta would listen to broadcasts from the Antenna above when they were young, on his very first radio.

They climb down to the basement, as Forty American planes drop their payloads on the city, one by one, in short succession, as the floor shakes to the core. They sleep. When they wake there is silence, this must be it. Time to hurry, to get Marie out. As they leave the house they enter a city in rubble, Werner takes her only so far, before he lets her go alone with a white pillowcase above her head. She puts something in his hand before she leaves, it is a big brass key.

After the last bomb has dropped the battle for Saint
Marlo is over. Etienne and Marie are reunited and do not
go back to Number 4 Vauborel.

Werner is picked up by Americans not far from Saint
Marlo and is taken to a processing house, but becomes
gravely ill, not able to keep down food, not able to eat.
He is sent to a field hospital where, others around him are
lifted to the sky daily.

One night as he feels there is nothing left of him, he
heads out of the field tent and into the grass nearby,
where he steps on a landmine, put there by his very own
army. He disappears in a mountain of earth.

Analysis
The crescendo of the story, ends here in Saint Marlo, as
the last bombs are dropped on the stronghold. Our
characters ordeals are over in a way and Werner feels like
he has offset his wrongs, by helping Marie. He dies at the
end of this part, but one senses with love in his heart and
not on the battle field.

Study Questions

1. Do you think Werner ran purposefully into the
   mines? If so, why?
2. How did you rate the ending? Would you have
   liked to Frausee Werner and Marie in a love story?
3. Why do you think Frank Volkheimer helped
   Werner to rescue Marie?

Quotations

"As shells scream over the house, he thinks only that he would like to sit there with her for a thousand years"

Part Eleven: 1945 Berlin

What Happens

Frau Elna and the last of the girls at the children's home, including Jutta are sent to Berlin to work in a factory. They work long days before the factory shuts and they are sent to do clean up in the streets. Bombings are still a nightly event, where they hide in the shelter at the end of their street.

The Germans are being defeated, disorder ensues and talks of the Russians and what they will do to the girls encircles the neighborhoods.

One night, they come to experience the barbaric ways of a colonel and three young sergeants as they rape them all one by one.

Jutta knows her brother is dead, buried somewhere in France. Years later she still remembers the Russian Colonel repeating what she thinks were the names of dead soldiers as he lay on top of her like a corpse.

Etienne and Marie return to Paris and live in the apartment she grew up in and every day her uncle scours the newspapers for news or whereabouts of her father.

They wait at the Gare de Auschwitz every afternoon as they watch the boys of not more than Eighteen years return from war. They look 80 years old, bags of bones, ghost like stares in their eyes.

He writes letters and the director of the museum promises they are doing everything they can to locate her father. There is no mention of the "Sea of Flames" stone.

Marie shares she would like to go to school.

Analysis

A short part, where we learn the tragic news of Jutta being raped by Russian soldiers after they go to work in the factories during the clean-up of Berlin.

The other young female character whose life has changed forever is Marie, now living back in Paris, where it all began. She never gives up hope of finding her father.

Study Questions

1. Why do you think the author included such a brutal ending scene for Jutta?
2. How do you think the aftermath of war affected everyone involved?
3. What was the role of women in the war?

Quotations

"The truth is that she is a disabled girl with no home and no parents"

Part Twelve: 1974

What Happens

It is 30 years since the end of World War II and Frank
Volkheimer lives in the suburbs of Pforzheim, Germany.
He is 51 years old. No children, no pets, not much at all
in his apartment, apart from a single chair in front of a
television set.

Volkheimer now fixes rooftop TV antennas for a living, a
possibly a gift inherited from his friend Werner. Life is
exhausting him and he is incredibly lonely. A lot of the
time he sees the eyes of the dead men he killed in his
mind's eye.

One day he receives a package in the post. Inside are
three pictures of items from the war. He recognizes
Werner's notebook immediately. The letter is seeking to
return items to next of kin and believe he would have
known the owner. He thinks back to how young the boy
was. Just a boy!

Jutta teaches, sixth grade algebra in Essen. She is married
and has a Six year old son. One day Volkheimer turns up
at her door with Werner's possessions. He retells stories
about where they were stationed and that he last saw
Werner in Saint Marlo where they were stationed for a
month, by the sea, he hints possibly he was in love.

For many years she has pushed the memories of war, the
awful last months in Berlin deep inside her. She doesn't

speak of her brother who got sent to a Hitler Youth Academy. She almost wants Volkheimer to leave and take the items with him.

She removes the items from his duffel bag, one by one. A diary wrapped in paper, a small carved wooden house. Jutta and her son Max make a journey to Saint Marlo. They enjoy the sea, the emerald sea, Werner wrote home about, that he wished his sister could see and now she is.

She asks about the wooden house in the museum, maybe it was from the town she thinks. A man recognizes the house as number 4 rue Vauborel, and takes them there. It is now apartments of course.

Marie-Laure LeBlanc manages a small laboratory at the Museum of Natural History in Paris. She traveled around with her uncle Etienne, who died peacefully in a bathtub aged eighty Three, leaving her lots of money.

They were never able to locate her father, even after spending thousands of Francs on private detectives. His last know location was noted in a German camp infirmary in which it states he had fever.

Marie has a daughter who is nineteen from a fling she had with a Canadian man named John. Helena her daughter, John and herself have dinner every Friday.

One day Jutta turns up at her work, with the wooden house. She asks about her brother and Marie reaffirms that he saved her life three times over and he was good in the face of Evil.

Fredrick still lives with his mother. The doctors say he will never have memories. One morning a letter comes with two pages of birds inside. It was a letter from Werner to Fredrick. It seems to bring back partial memory and he speaks, which he has not done in years.

Analysis

We round up all of the important people Werner came into contact with in his short life. Jutta has put her memories of her brother aside and feels slight anger that Volkheimer comes to re-stir these feelings. This is a scene which helps to put things to bed. Left over pieces of the jigsaw if you like. After all the destruction of the war, it is important to see the life's of our characters lead a seemingly normal life.

Study Questions

1. Why do you think Jutta doesn't keep the Diamond, once she sees it in the box?
2. How can having Werner's things help put feelings to rest for Marie and Jutta?

Quotations

Volkheimer paces in the harsh dazzle of the billboard lights and feels his loneliness on him like a disease.

Part Thirteen: 2014

What Happens

Marie still lives and is in Paris, where she grew up and has lived most of her life. She walks with her 12 year old Grandson as he plays war games on a handheld computer. He walks with her every Wednesday evening.

The world is a changed place. Communication travels all around her, way up high above the city, on emails, mobiles phones, texts. Maybe the souls of Werner, her father and Uncle Etienne float along with them.

She counts the storm drains "One Storm drain, then two and three" until they reach her building. They say "good bye" and agree to meet again next week.

She listens till his footsteps fade and all she can hear is the hum of the traffic, of Paris.

Analysis

The closing scene, we see Marie walking with her grandson, two generations from her. He plays pretend war games, as she quietly reflects what it is to be in a real war. She doesn't talk with him about war.

Everything is moving quickly around her, communication is more than radio broadcasts, it's fast and up in the air, with her memories of Etienne and her father. She knows the streets of Paris like the back of her hand and the noises she hears now instead of planes and bombs are the hum of traffic.

Study Questions

1. How do you think young people in 2014 relate to war?

2. Is it somehow irresponsible to have war games, as a plaything?

3. How can the younger generation learn more about the wars that happened not so long ago?

Critical Reviews

If reviews of Doerr's book were solely based on his
storytelling abilities, I think you may be hard pushed to
find a critic who wouldn't agree that "All The Light You
Cannot See" is a beautiful piece of prose and a masterly
crafted piece of storytelling, in which Doerr takes the
setting of World War II and turns it into the backdrop for
a "relentless" bash on all your senses. The descriptions in
Doerr's book are so detailed, it is agreed you really have
a sensory overload when reading.

That said the critics are quick to highlight Doerr's
technical Inadequacies as a writer, which had the story
not been so compelling would have changed their overall
view of this book.

The story swings between France and Germany during
and before, World War II. Whilst also flitting between
time frames of before, during and after the War.

The events told mostly through the eyes of our main
characters Werner Pfennig and Marie Le Blanc, develop
fast as the bombers start to drop their payloads on the
walled city of Saint Marlo, one of Germans last
strongholds.

Although the main characters' stories run parallel to each
other, you are always in anticipation to know, when will
Marie and Werner cross paths? When the pair eventually
meet in the last part before the end of the book, some
people agree they feel let down as there isn't more about
their relationship and what it could be. This I would say

is a symbol of how touched a person of the war could be, by just a chance meeting.

Doerr's attention to detail is infectious and critics agree that it is this detail which draws the reader into the world of the story and allows you to become emotionally attached to the characters' predicaments.

The pace and length of the book are up for debate. Some believe it is too long as a piece of prose, at 530 pages, even though the action does move rapidly. Some critics ask for more content when it comes to the historical accuracy and more of a world centered on what it was like "Really" to live in France or Germany during the war?

All critics agree that Marie's character, is complete, more so than Werner's and Marie's blindness convincing and a great symbol of the people who choose to ignore the evil happening on their doorstep.

The overall feeling is that Doerr didn't create a historically accurate book, dealing with the brutal regime of the Third Reich, but a fictional tale, a future Hollywood blockbuster, maybe, where history is distorted with Americanism and unflawed characters like Fredrick exist.

The New York Times sums up the thoughts of many a critic by stating "Doerr's novel is more than a thriller, less than a piece of literature and what is known amongst English folk as a good read or a great page turner."

Although the New York Times, also gives Doerr the

accolade of stating that his book Is one of the most important pieces of fiction of 2014. So a contradictory critic from the same publication.

Final Thoughts

It was hard to put this book down. The action is gripping and you can't help but feel you are in the mist of the scenes with surround sound. By flitting between past and present Doerr, allows his wartime story to escalate at great speed, creating a huge sense of tension.

The main action around the city of Saint Marlo represents one of those key battleground fights in World War II where the Germans fought till the bitter end. Marie's characters being blind, gives way to the development of a sound scape, which is evident all the way through the book.

You do feel at times that you can sense the Americanisms of the Author and that the two main characters are in fact Europeans. More of a feeling of heritage and custom from that point, would have been great and less use of modern Americanized language. I sometimes didn't feel this was the war time 1945 battle ground we were on, but possibly the 1990 Gulf War.

This is not a history book, but more a sensorineural guide to the loud machine of war. The story is filled to the brim with sensory triggers and you feel like you could be part of that big noise. Yes the language is loud, it is not a cute book about a small town girl, but a city girl and she survives of an even louder battle; The War!

My overall thoughts are that although Werner and Marie were not meant to spend too much time together, we don't really get a grasp of how Marie's character feels about the man who saved her life.

I personally would remember him forever.

Glossary

Daniel Le Blanc: Marie's father
Dr. Hauptmann: Professor at Werner's school
Etienne: Marie's Uncle
Frank Volkheimer: A German Sargent
Frau Elena: The nun who runs the children's home
Fredrick: Werner's friend from School
Jutter: Werner's younger sister
Marie-Laure Le Blanc: A young French blind girl and protagonist of the story.
Madame Manec: House Keeper at Etienne's home.
Sergeant Major Reinhold Von Rumpel: German Colonel
Werner Pfennig: A German boy and protagonist of the story
Sea of Flames: A precious stone, with a cursed past.
Zollverein: A mining complex in Germany

Recommended Reading

About Grace (2005)

Doerr's second published book, a novel entitles "About Grace" has been regarded as a beautiful piece of prose, with the same painstaking attention to detail that is Doerr's trademark.

It centers on a hydrologist named David Winkler, whose dreams sometimes become a reality. David is from Alaska and has a slight obsession with snow and snowflakes. Sometimes David dreams things which come true, which is a gift he is not ready to receive and flees his family and home to deny his future and the dreams of reality and ends up destitute on a beach in The Caribbean, where a family take him under their wing and try to reel him back into the world.

 This book tries to deal with the frailty of humans and question the effects of nature on the human condition, the nature of family and the natural worlds around us.

The book tries to ask questions about snowflakes, predetermination, the nature of family, and the intersections of the human and natural worlds. It takes place in Alaska, the Caribbean, Ohio, and plenty of places in between.

Doerrs second award winning novel has been described as a luminous piece of prose, "heartbreaking and astonishingly accomplished"

The Shell Collector (2002)

These short stories are Doerr's debut collection and take readers from the coasts of Africa, the forest of Montana, cold wet moors of Lapland and beyond. Many of these places Doerr has visited or even lived for a period of time, so this adds to the intricate exploration of these physical and emotional landscapes. Regarding as a "Show stopping Debut" by critics, Doerr's Prose is bursting with finite natural beauty and profound meaning often lost in the modern American short story.

Each story explores the magnificence of the human condition in all its guises; love, grief, fractured relationships, metamorphosis and opens it up so Natures power and abundance. Each story has a character who experiences these big emotions and a connection to the big universe beyond their own.

Other Recommended Reading

Memory Wall: Anthony Doerr **(2010)**

Four Seasons in Rome: On Twins, Insomnia and the Biggest Funeral in the History of the World: Anthony Doerr **(2007)**

Life After Life: Kate Atkinson **(2013)**

Made in the USA
Lexington, KY
24 July 2015